Salty
the Sea Turtle

Written by Claire Lawrence

Illustrated by Randi Zwicker

First published by Dog Ear Publishing
4011 Vincennes Road
Indianapolis, IN 46268
www.dogearpublishing.net

ISBN: 978-1-4575-3304-4

This book is a work of fiction. Places, events, and situations in this book are purely
fictional and any resemblance to actual persons, living or dead, is coincidental.

This book is printed on acid free paper.
Printed in the United States of America

This book is dedicated to the park ranger who gave us the rare opportunity to witness the hatching of a baby sea turtle and to all the men and women who have devoted their lives to the preservation of this amazing creature.

The mother spends
hours building her nest,

Making sure it will be
a safe place.

Burying her eggs deep in
the sand,

Then disappearing with-
out a trace.

Months go by until the time is right,

Inside the little egg Salty grew.

Four fins, two eyes, a
shell, and a tail,

Crackle, crackle! Oh no!
It's time to push through!

The sky is filled with
twinkling stars,

The moon shines bright in the night.

9

Up through the sand her little fins pop,

Excited and filled with delight!

Following a path by the light of the moon,

Leading her safe to the sea.

Catching a ride on the tip of a wave,

At last Salty's finally free!

Floating on a carpet of greenish seaweed

Out into the ocean so deep.

Filling her belly with shrimp and fish,

Then drifting off to sleep.

Farther and farther,
Salty goes on her way,

Her life's journey has just begun.

Dolphins, fish, and manatees,

What could be more fun?

Time passes slowly living out in the sea,

Salty grows bigger and bigger each day.

Knowing that someday she will return to the beach,

Was still many years away.

Salty travels to places both near and far,

Swimming in and out with the tide.

Some days are sunny and some days are cloudy,

To be expected in an ocean so wide.

Salty knows she will build a nest of her own,

Filled with eggs of brown and white.

More tiny turtles will swim out to sea,

By the glow of the pale moonlight.

The day finally arrives
when Salty swims home,

Returning to the beach of her birth.

Carefully picking her favorite spot,

She begins digging into the earth.

With her eggs safely tucked down deep in the sand,

Salty turns toward the ocean so blue.

Making her way back into the sea,

Salty has done what she was born to do.

Did you know?

- Salty is called a "loggerhead turtle." She is this type of turtle because of her large head and strong jaw.

- Salty uses her jaw for feeding, cracking the hard shells of the food she eats such as shrimp and shellfish.

- Loggerhead turtles weigh about three hundred pounds and can be up to four feet long.

- The nest a loggerhead makes is called a "clutch."

- Females lay more than a hundred ping-pong ball-sized eggs in their clutch.

- A female may lay as many as four clutches a year. It takes sixty days for a loggerhead egg to hatch.

- A baby sea turtle is called a "hatchling."

- When baby loggerheads swim out to sea, it is called a "swimming frenzy." Each baby turtle covers up to one mile per hour!

- Only one female in every one thousand baby turtles survives to return back to the beach where she was born.

- The female loggerhead digs her nest in the sand and lays her eggs at night.

- The male loggerheads live in the sea their entire lives.

- The loggerhead can live close to sixty years. Some have been known to live even longer.

The End

CPSIA information can be obtained
at www.ICGtesting.com
Printed in the USA
LVOW05s1931040117
519750LV00003B/4/P